Metaphorosis

December 2018

Beautifully made speculative fiction

Metaphorosis

December 2018

edited by
B. Morris Allen

Metaphorosis Books

Neskowin

ISSN: 2573-136X (online)
ISBN: 978-1-64076-122-3 (e-book)
ISBN: 978-1-64076-123-0 (paperback)

December 2018

Of Hair and Beanstalks

William Condon

25 December, being the Birth-day of Isaac Newton, Physicist:

Madam,

Your stepdaughter has arrived and been installed in the tower chamber, per your instructions. This has already led to the predicted difficulties, as my dinosaurian bulk cannot fit within the narrow tower. When she refused to descend for supper this evening, I was reduced to flying outside her window and poking my face in.

I found her combing her long hair, which raises my second concern: while I am ill-acquainted with human customs, your instructions to periodically observe her appear to overstep the bounds of propriety. However, as you are not only her stepmother but a human noblelady yourself, I shall bow to your procedural knowledge.

Most dutifully,
ANTRODEMOS, Dinosaur.

27 December, being the Birth-day of Johannes Kepler, Astronomer and loyal adviser to his king:

Madam,

While narrative is not my strength, as you have requested to hear the particulars of your stepdaughter's arrival, I shall attempt to recount them.

Her coach arrived shortly after the morning sun had burnt off the frost. It came as you described sending it: by the usual road, locked from the outside, and surrounded by six bodyguards. Upon the door's being unlatched in the courtyard of my castle, your stepdaughter disembarked with a sigh and addressed me in a despairing voice, "Mister Dragon, did Gothel send me here for you to eat me?"

I at once corrected her that (a) I am not a dragon but a dinosaur, for "dragon" is a word used in unreliable peasants' tales while "dinosaur" is a rigorous term used by modern scientists (and I know no more precise term of matching rigor that would correctly describe me); and (b) I do not eat humans.

She took these corrections with the dubious air I have observed from too many other persons, even in the nearby village. But, addressing me correctly as "dinosaur," she inquired of the conditions under which she was to live here. I replied with your specifications, to wit, that I was to "keep an eye on that Rapunzel every couple of hours, at least, to make sure she's not planning to escape or see any strange men – not that there're any wandering princes around your tower."

Although she appeared accepting in my presence, she was apparently unaware of my excellent dinosaurian hearing, for I later overheard her sobbing in her tower chamber.

Most dutifully,
ANTRODEMOS, Dinosaur.

*1 January, being the Commemoration of
Julius Caesar and Sosigenes Alexandris,
Calendarists, who were sadly forced to
give up Science for politics:*

Madam,

Your stepdaughter intruded upon my
workshop this morning while I was about
a most delicate experiment. When I
explained as much and ordered her to
depart, she pertly replied that as I had
been "peering at" her all week, she had
rights to do the same to me. I replied that
you had appointed me to supervise her.
She refused response save to appropriate
one of my human-sized chairs and say I
"might as well continue."

Since forcibly removing her would be a
greater disruption to the experiment than
tolerating her presence, I did continue.
However, I fear my measurement of the
gases emitted is imprecise, since my
attention was repeatedly distracted by
your stepdaughter's fidgeting. I shall have

to obtain further phosphates — and while that will not be hard, I fear what would result if she repeats this during next month's planned analysis of platinum, a rare and expensive metal from distant lands.

Fortunately, further interference was forestalled by the arrival of one of the local delivery-boys. I was (or, more precisely, my servants were) pleased to obtain further preserved vegetables and fresh milk; the boy also brought the soil samples I had requested from his farm. (A vascular stem plant of highly unusual height had grown there the previous autumn; I was unfortunately unable to study it before it was cut down and burnt.) It is fortunate there is no snow in this locale as there is farther north; that would greatly impede this sampling. Your stepdaughter, to my great satisfaction, remained in the courtyard for the rest of the morning.

Most dutifully,
ANTRODEMOS, Dinosaur.

2 January, being the Birth-day of Johann Titius, Astronomer and Taxonomist:

Madam,

As you have demanded an immediate response, I write in haste.

Your stepdaughter indeed remained in the company of Jack, the delivery-boy, for between one and two hours before (the gatekeeper reports) he expressed a need to return to his farm.

Being personally unaware of his reputation in our environs, I asked the castle cooks. They were at first unwilling to tell me, but finally reported that his name is Jack, his father died approximately two years ago, and he currently keeps farm with his mother (named Mildred). While his reputation has been besmirched with accusations of laziness and poor financial dealings, he has recently come into money and has hired hands to perform delayed maintenance on the farm. Further, he has always been acknowledged for his courage.

I regret that I cannot add to this testimony personally. Most of the neighboring farmers are frightened to speak with a dinosaur such as myself, no matter how often I reassure them I am not a dragon. Perhaps it would help if I introduced myself by a more precise taxonomic term than "dinosaur"? Sadly, I cannot tell which genus of dinosaur I would best be categorized under. None of the published descriptions of specific dinosaur genera fit me well, the Academy has not answered my letters asking for clarification, and I hesitate to create a new term by myself. In the meantime, the local farmers and villagers remain unacquainted with the delights of Science, and I am forced to interview my reluctant servants about Jack's reputation.

Regardless, I reassure you I have indeed been periodically inspecting your stepdaughter's room, as instructed. The customs of human nobility are difficult to understand, but as your castellan, I will comply and (I hope) eventually comprehend.

Most dutifully,

ANTRODEMOS, Dinosaur.

5 January, being the Birth-day of Xu Xiake, Geographer:

Madam,

I indeed agree that (even from my limited knowledge) Master Jack seems an ill match for your stepdaughter. However, might it not be an overreaction to forbid her from seeing any young men? Does not understanding come from experiment? Still, as I know some experiments bear overly high risks, I will comply.

Be that as it may, I roundly rejected her proposal of yesterday to hold "a dance, or a feast, or at least something" in honor of Twelfth Night as a frivolous gaiety which would distract from Science. "But you're a dragon," she replied. "Dragons might be that glum, but I'm not!" I again corrected her that I am a dinosaur, and invited her to join me in the mysteries of experimentation. Instead, she left for her tower, and I have not seen her since (save through the window, as per your instructions.)

Master Jack will next be coming on the ninth, as per his normal schedule.

Most dutifully,
ANTRODEMOS, Dinosaur.

10 January, being the Anniversary of Thomas Savery's inventing a smooth paddle-wheel:

Madam,

As your stepdaughter has continued protesting boredom, I decided to commemorate the date by a lecture on fluid dynamics. Sadly, despite my best attempts, both she and the castle servants appeared impatient. Finally, amid a discussion of the specific gravity of common air over different temperatures, she interrupted, "Can we use that paddle-wheel? Go boating?"

Taken aback, I protested the local stream was much too small — but I could demonstrate another invention of Captain Savery's: an engine powered by steam. She immediately agreed, and the visibly-curious servants helped us assemble the needed vessels and tubes. I lit the fire with my dinosaurian breath, and we watched the engine spurt water across the courtyard. It was a simple demonstration, but they seemed surprisingly engrossed.

Just after I had increased the fire (again at your stepdaughter's urging) and the engine started squirting water over the castle wall, Master Jack arrived bearing food. Your stepdaughter eagerly told him all about the engine, but after a few minutes (bearing in mind both your instructions, and her inaccuracies in attempting to explain the principles behind it) I drew him away into a longer discussion of gas dynamics. He attempted to follow, but was sadly ignorant of that science's mathematical foundations. I showed him out after approximately a half-hour.

Meanwhile, I overheard my servants wondering to each other whether I planned to set fire to the village to build more steam engines. I reminded them that I am no dragon but a dinosaur, and your castellan. They did not seem to be reassured, but I know not what else to say to them.

Most dutifully,
ANTRODEMOS, Dinosaur.

13 January, being the Anniversary of King Henry's Ban on Purported Transmutation of Metals:

Madam,

I must protest your interdict. I am not a dragon; just as I will not burn down villages, I will not hold maidens hostage for no rational reason or custom. I am a dinosaur, and a scientist. You have entrusted me with this castle, and you have charged me to keep watch on Rapunzel, so I will follow your instructions regarding her even though they be confusing and distasteful. Yet I will explain Science to whomever I wish: to Jack, if he wishes, or anyone else.

To my surprise, two days after my demonstration, Rapunzel asked me to teach her Science. I attempted to start her on gas dynamics, but as it did not hold her interest (nor had she the necessary math), we swiftly moved to mechanics. It appears that human fingers are much more versatile than dinosaurian claws; we have been able to measure the velocity of marbles after collisions with much greater precision than I could beforehand.

I hope this may distract Rapunzel from her ill-advised romance and convince the villagers that there is more to Science than lighting fires.

Most dutifully,
ANTRODEMOS, Dinosaur.

16 January, being the Anniversary of the Publication of an Organized Grammar by Elio Antonio de Nebrija, Linguist:

Madam,

Jack again arrived bearing foodstuffs, as normal. I met him at the gate, where (despite the suspicious glances I saw from some of the servants and passers-by), we passed a pleasant hour discussing physics before again being stymied by his sad lack of math. To my surprise, though, he suggested that next week I begin remedying that lack — a suggestion which I gladly accepted.

However, after I left, I am informed that Rapunzel passed some words with him inside the gatehouse (where she had been hiding) before the gatekeeper's arrival caused her to fall silent.

Before our normal physics lesson later that day, I asked Rapunzel what they had said. She refused to respond; I thought it futile to press her. Per your orders, I have cautioned the gatekeeper against a repeat.

Most dutifully,

ANTRODEMOS, Dinosaur.

22 January, being the Birth-day of Francis Bacon, staunch defender of personal observation:

Madam,

As instructed, Jack did not come to the castle today. Instead, I visited him at his farm. After reassuring his mother that I was not a dragon but a dinosaur (sadly, she did not appear to be reassured), we went out into the fields for a somewhat-satisfactory math lesson. He did not even mention Rapunzel, and the neighboring farmers who were eyeing us with unease looked relieved at my departure.

Meanwhile, Rapunzel herself continues to repeat physics experiments with me, but she refuses to analyze any results unless I work through them with her. I continue to fly outside her window as instructed, and to the best of my knowledge, she has not seen Jack since last week.

Most dutifully,
ANTRODEMOS, Dinosaur.

25 January, being the Birth-day of Robert
Boyle, who clarified the nature of
Chemistry by clearly delineating elements:

Madam,
I am not a dragon, but a dinosaur. Dinosaurs do not eat humans. Nor has Jack done anything deserving eating; he is a surprisingly apt student who has (despite your suspicions) engaged in no importune behavior.
Most clearly,
ANTRODEMOS, Dinosaur.

31 January, being the Death-day of Jost
Burgi, Mathematician:

Madam,
I have indeed received your letters, and I am disturbed by how you continue to emphasize one subject and even descend to threats. While this castle does belong to you, I remain and shall remain an

honorable dinosaur and scientist. I was under the impression we both understood this when I became your castellan?

I regret to report that, while doing my inspection last night, Rapunzel leaned out her window to lambast my "horrid suspicions" and "leering glare" which was "always watching" her. I apologized, saying that I was only following your orders; she replied that she would not study Science with me anymore and retreated glumly to her bed.

Thinking back, I am unaware what might have prompted such behavior, as nothing has changed from the last week.

I suppose you will be satisfied to hear that I did discover a rope ladder in her room; I burnt it despite loud objections.

Yours,
ANTRODEMOS, Dinosaur.

6 February, being the Birth-day of Scipio del Ferro, who solved puzzles in Mathematics:

Madam,

No, my silence does not mean I am conspiring with Rapunzel against you. Rather, there is nothing to report. Rapunzel has holed herself up in her room save for meals. She has apparently attempted gardening — I found the remains of strange vines under her window and have taken samples for future study.

Meanwhile, Master Jack has (despite your insinuations) not been in the castle, nor spoken with Rapunzel. I flew to meet him at his farm yesterday, where he continues to study Science diligently, belying his reputed laziness.

I might mention that I saw one of your Message-Men delivering Jack's mother a letter as I was approaching the farm. Since they were eyeing Jack and me with fear later on, I venture the opinion that your letter did not have its desired result?

Yours,

ANTRODEMOS, Dinosaur.

9 February, being the Death-day of Giulio Vanini, Natural Philosopher

Madam,

You will, no doubt, be reassured that Master Jack's mother has forbidden his return to this castle.

I was surprised when I saw Mistress Mildred bringing today's delivery instead of her son. She instantly fell to the ground when I approached her, eventually stammering (after much encouragement from me) that she "thought he really shouldn't dare" come here anymore. To my further inquiries, she added that I "should know really well why." As I did not wish to terrify her further, I let her go.

I fear someone is planning something, but I do not know what — and I do not know what experiments would show me the answer.

Yours,
ANTRODEMOS, Dinosaur

11 February, being the Death-day of René Descartes, who founded philosophy on doubt:

Madam,

To my shame, I confess my investigations were insufficient. This very evening, I discovered Jack in Rapunzel's room, his having accessed it via another rope ladder. He and Rapunzel were talking, apparently about some ball or feast.

I interrupted their conversation by sticking my head in the window. They both immediately fell to the floor screaming and begging me not to burn them alive. I replied that I would neither burn my own castle nor kill humans needlessly, and demanded to know how long they had been seeing each other.

Rapunzel babbled that this was the first time, but Jack immediately said he had been coming every few days since late January. I thanked him for his honesty but ordered him to leave at once, which he did.

I see now that not only have my investigations been insufficient (for I missed Jack's presence), but so has my understanding of their characters. I have planted myself atop Rapunzel's tower for the present, where I shall meditate on this. I also await whatever advice you may have to give.

Yours,

ANTRODEMOS, Dinosaur.

*13 February, being the Anniversary of
Galileo Galilei's arrival to stand trial by
those who protested how he presented
Science*

Madam,

I do not know how or whether this letter will reach you, unless I fly it on my own dinosaurian wings. Perhaps, should the besiegers triumph, one of them will send it with a letter asking for you to send a better and more human castellan. And, if they are correct in their claims, perhaps you will be glad to see their letter.

I find that hard to believe — did you not pledge your friendship to me? Did you not welcome me as the hoped-upon herald of future dinosaurs joining society and Science? Have I not been your good castellan these years? It is that which holds me back inside these walls: that a good castellan would not use his claws and fiery breath upon his people, nor a good scientist upon his neighbors. Thus, I wait in anxious hope that you will rescue me.

Yet the mob of farmers and villagers outside shout from outside every wall that you support them; that you have sent them letters asking them to rise against me as if I were a vicious dragon (I use the vulgar term by intent); that I am luring Jack to devour him; that my very silence proves my guilt and shame. I know Mistress Mildred did receive some letter from you, but surely she is misrepresenting it?

I have not sent out the few human guards, for they would be outnumbered; it seems every villager has come out in arms. I could fly out myself, but would that not prove their claims that I am no civilized scientist and unfit to join society? But if I continue to do nothing, would not the castle you have entrusted me be lost?

Your stepdaughter, I fear, does not share my doubts. She shrugs off the siege, saying that one captor will be no worse than another. And human politics are beyond me; might it be she is correct? But when I asked her to teach me of politics, she ordered me out, saying she needed to wash her hair.

As I reflect on the strange letters you have recently sent me, I wonder how much of the customs of human society I have failed to understand?

Yours in confusion,
ANTRODEMOS, Dinosaur

14 February, being the Birth-day of Georg Fuchsel, Geologist, who studied records written in rock many ages ago:

Madam,

I cannot but wonder how many letters will pile up unsent before this castle is overrun.

Meantimes, I underestimated Rapunzel's ingenuity and both her and Jack's dedication. While looking out toward her tower this rainy evening, a lightning flash illuminated it enough for me to see (with my dinosaurian eyes) a human shape climbing up from the siege lines!

I instantly flew over. It was Jack, climbing up a plant that had somehow grown in mere hours. I cut it with a thwack of my tail, meaning to catch Jack in his fall, but Rapunzel threw down her hair with a scream, and Jack grabbed onto it. He was too heavy for her to pull him up, however; I caught him in midair and growled "What is this?"

But he was unconscious.

I then flew up to Rapunzel, who was trying to haul in her waterlogged hair and massage her doubtlessly-aching neck. Her face white, she pleaded, "Don't send me back! Don't send me to my stepmother!"

I demanded why she did this. "Because I needed to!" she answered. I attempted to explain the difference between necessity and free will, but she interrupted, "I love him!"

Seeing the futility of further conversation, and not noticing any activity from the siege lines, I flew down to deposit Jack in the infirmary and write this letter. I am again at a loss as to what to do. Even my shipment of platinum for experiments is now unable to reach me. Perhaps it would have been better had you entrusted this castle to a human in the first place?

Yours in great confusion,
ANTRODEMOS, Dinosaur.

15 February, being the Birth-day of Galileo Galilei, Astronomer:

Madam,

As Jack has singlehandedly lifted the siege, I now give him my wholehearted recommendation as a fitting match for your stepdaughter.

Rapunzel met me before dawn this morning outside the infirmary, pleading for me to be kind to Jack. Still disturbed, I said I could not make any promises and reminded her that he had rebelled against his liege lady (you) and her castellan (myself). In response, she claimed you had indeed urged them to rebel, and made many other claims about you that I scarce would have credited two months ago. However, your recent letters' single-minded focus on keeping Rapunzel securely enclosed and watched makes her claims sadly plausible: that none of your instructions concerning her are ordinary, that you are accustomed to lose trust in anyone who is not cooperating with your watch of her, and that you would stir up any matter of rumors to keep young men away from Rapunzel.

I scarce would credit such claims normally — but have not these last months given as good evidence toward them as any experiment?

Shaken, I promised to keep an open mind about Jack, and we entered.

He was awake, and reading a mathematics book I had ordered left for him. Setting it down, he stared at me without words. When I reminded him of our collaborations in Science, he accused me of holding Rapunzel prisoner. I told him I was merely following your express instructions; he protested "Then don't! You shouldn't keep her cooped up here anyway! Does her stepmother want her held captive like a dragon's pet princess?"

I must confess I was shaken by this and asked him what to do.

Jack proposed an experiment: I would let him go, and if he ended the siege, then I would set Rapunzel free. That plan, Rapunzel added, would let me discharge my duty to you by keeping your castle intact.

Reluctantly, I saw that both other courses would have me acting like a dragon in one way or another. At a loss for what else to do, I expressed doubts that he could end the siege, but agreed.

"Don't worry," he said casually. Apparently, his stealth had been sufficient to slay a murderous giant earlier in the fall (whose castle he had accessed by climbing up a bean plant of unusual height.) "Just observe, like you said scientists should, right?"

I followed him and Rapunzel up to the battlements, where he waved his hands and announced to the now-silent crowds outside that I did not wish to act as a dragon, and that I would willingly let both him and Rapunzel go and promise never to hurt anyone without cause. The assailants replied, asking what proof I offered of this, and accusing me of planning to burn them all for my new steam engine.

At that, Jack laughed. "It was a human who invented that steam engine!" he exclaimed. "And this dinosaur's science can give you a lot of other good inventions, too! Right?"

Thereupon he turned to me, and I had nothing else to do but nod my head.

The crowd murmured in confusion, but they were evidently calmed, and some were throwing down their improvised weapons.

Jack then ordered the gates thrown open, and (with me observing) he and Rapunzel strode out to the crowd.

As I write this less than an hour later, I am still wondering if I did wrong. My trust in you is lessened — but did not experiment point in that direction? I did violate your instructions — but what else could I have done save act like a dragon and prove my enemies right? I did lose control of the situation — but is that not part of joining society?

Yours in even greater confusion,
ANTRODEMOS, Dinosaur

16 February, being the Birth-day of Georg Rheticus, who spread the truth of Astronomy

Madam,

I am pleased that we are finally once more in correspondence. Your letter clarified everything wonderfully. No, I shall not throw Rapunzel in the dungeons, nor shall I devour Jack, nor shall I do any of the other evil things you were insinuating I might do in the letters you wrote Mistress Mildred and the other townspeople (which letters they recently showed me.) Their earlier behavior was improper, but they do not deserve any grave punishment: Rapunzel, I now see, was reacting to her unjust imprisonment; and Jack is unaware of nobles' etiquette and unfortunately prejudiced against dinosaurs.

Therefore, I will not re-imprison Jack or Rapunzel. They are currently at Jack's house having luncheon with his mother, and they are already talking of betrothal. While I personally think this is far too hasty, I will no longer attempt to discourage them.

Further, Jack is showing no laziness in his scientific studies: he is already talking of double-checking the farm's boundaries using trigonometry and studying methods to improve the soil's health before the next planting. He has also given me new inspiration in my experiments — I have recently sent orders to sell the platinum and buy materials to study better farming. The recent siege showed I can no longer merely observe society; if I am to act, I shall act as a good scientist who uses Science for a purpose.

Perhaps farming is not the best career for Jack in the long run? If so, marrying a noblelady such as Rapunzel would not be unfitting.

Yours in Science and good sense,
ANTRODEMOS, Dinosaur.

*William Condon's story "Of Hair and
Beanstalks" was published in Metaphorosis on
Friday, 7 December 2018.*

About the story

"Of Hair and Beanstalks" merged three ideas I'd been pondering for a while. First, I'd been playing with the idea of a dragon who wanted to join society - how would people treat him? What kind of person would he be to do that? Then, I'd been wondering how the villains in fairy tales might try to justify themselves to their supporters. And, finally, I love the history of science and how it's dramatically changed the world over the last centuries. When I decided Antrodemos joined society because of that, almost everything fell into place for the story.

A question for the author

Q: When do you decide a story is finished?

A: When I first get through to "The End," I set the story aside and mull over how to fix the points I'm not satisfied with. Sometimes I can put my finger on the problems at once and how to fix them; other times I know something's wrong but need some time to puzzle out what. Then, I revise. I hardly ever agree a story's perfect, but there's a point where I know it's good and I don't know how to make it any better - and that's when I decide it's finished.

About the author

William Condon is a writer and programmer. He lives outside Seattle where he enjoys cycling and dreaming up new worlds.

I Will Go Gently

Susan McDonough-Wachtman

They sat in their deck chairs, watching their son fish. "Has he caught one?" she asked, gently rocking.

Walter squinted out at the lake. "I don't think so."

"I think he did."

"Did you *see* it?" Ellen had the sight, but to Walter's constant exasperation, she made no distinction between things she saw and things she *saw*.

"No."

He looked at her. Her eyes were on her knitting. "How could you know, Ellen? You're not even looking at him."

"I just know."

"Hogwash." He resumed his contemplation of the lake. He pointed. "A coupla loons." He glanced over at her and saw her half smile. "I didn't say *we* were the loons."

Her smile widened. "Did you see the otter?" She pointed with her needle.

"No. Where? Now?" He looked where she indicated.

"No, this morning, early."

"Why didn't you say so?" Fifty years they had been married and still she didn't tell him things right away. She said it wasn't necessary, because he could see *back*, but still. He made a swiping motion with his hand and looked into the space he had made, a little viewpoint into the past. His heavy features lightened with pleasure. "Huh. You're right. Good, maybe there are more." He watched for a moment, hopefully. They had moved to inland Nunavut to escape the rising sea but had worried about the spread of pollution from the flooded cities. It was still a concern, twenty years later, but an increase in the otter population would be a good sign. "Mmm. Don't see others." Disappointed, he closed the vision with a wave. "How did you see it? You don't get up that early."

"I do lately."

"Hogwash. You've never been a morning person."

"I sleep very lightly these days, Walter."

He looked at her, frowning, worried. "Hog—"

"—wash, I know." She smiled again, a gentle creasing of her wrinkles. "I know you don't want me to die. But I'm not afraid."

"I am." He muttered it low, but she heard.

Her eyes went back to her knitting. "You'll be fine."

He stood abruptly and slammed his hands against the railing. He winced. His hands weren't as tough as they used to be. And his leg ached. He had broken it falling off the barn roof. She had warned him not to go up there.

"Have you *seen* me fall?" he had asked her.

"No, I just saw a shadow over you."

"Well, I'm not going to leave the roof unfixed because of a shadow."

Now he was using a cane and probably would for the rest of his life. His leg hurt. He was no use to anyone. Getting old was shitty.

They had both aged quickly these last twenty years. They had left the benefits of society behind and had survived with hard work but insufficient health care — just like any other pioneers. Someday, she said, more people with gifts of power would be born into their little community, including seers and healers. Their Inuit-related tribe had always produced them, but sporadically, and no one knew how or why. Their own son was "ungifted" and apparently content to be so.

"I think Julian's coming back."

"Oh, good, fish for dinner." She set her knitting in the basket at her feet. She knitted only a few minutes at a time these days before her hands cramped and she had to stop. "Do you remember when we moved here? You said he'd never be happy out here at the end of the world."

"And he wouldn't have been, if Penny hadn't come." She had *seen* the others coming, but she hadn't been sure there would be someone for Julian. The visions of seers were sporadic, uncontrollable, and sometimes unreliable. The future could be changed. "But she did, and they'll be marrying soon. They'll have children."

"Have you *seen* it?" He looked down at her frizzy white hair. Her thin, veined brown fingers were like the driftwood twigs on the saltwater beach where they had grown up. That beach had long since disappeared under a rising sea. It had been Ellen and the other seers who had warned their people first, even before the scientists from Down Below. But many had chosen not to listen. Just as he had chosen not to listen to her warning about working on the roof. If you put your hands over your ears and said, "la la la," all the bad news would go away.

"Some things I know without seeing," she said.

He barked out a laugh, startling the birds in the garden. "You don't know. You just — you're just — an infernal optimist."

She giggled. That sound took him back. He swiped at the air and smiled at his memory of her, sitting on another deck, long ago, her hair a thick, dark mass caught into a long braid down her back, her slim, clever hands busy making a dreamcatcher.

"Come back here," she ordered, in the present.

"Why? Why should I?" He rubbed off the tear running down his cheek. With a wave of his hand, he dismissed his hovering vision of the past.

"Because I am still here. And because he needs you."

He looked down at the beach, where their son was tying the boat up to the dock. "Don't be silly. He's done that by himself since he was ten. Besides, I'm no help to him these days." He tapped the cane hanging on the railing beside him.

She shook her head. "I don't mean right now. I mean when I'm gone."

"What about me?" He knew he sounded childish. He couldn't stop himself. He stared out at the water, not wanting to face her.

She sighed. "It won't be long —" He could hear the creak of her chair as she shifted.

"Please stop saying that."

"Let me finish."

The snap in her voice took him by surprise. He turned around.

"I was going to say," she continued, "it won't be long before you join me."

His hands gripped the railing behind him. He was younger than she was, and stronger, and healthier. His mouth opened, but he couldn't get any words past his teeth. Everything he thought to say got stuck there, like gristle.

She was looking up at him, calm again, with that calm which had always infuriated and delighted him. At many of the worst times in their years together, she had regarded him with just that expression of peace and a faint sense of humor. He always got the impression she was laughing at him, just a little. He hated it. He loved it.

"I haven't told you before," she said softly, "because I wasn't sure if it would help."

"What ..." He cleared his throat, turned and spat over the railing. "What do you mean by that?"

"Will you miss me enough to be glad to die?"

Silence for a moment while they both listened to these words, and felt them weighing down the air between them.

"Glad to die? Why would anyone be glad to die?"

"I am." She smiled sadly. "I'm tired and in pain all the time. You know this."

"Yes, but —"

"I know. You want me to 'rage.' But, you see, I know the light isn't dying." She waited a moment. "We can talk about this later, if you want to."

"If I want to? If I *want* to?"

Their son came up to the porch, carrying his basket of fish. He considered each of their faces in turn and sighed. "You've upset him again, Mother." He bent down and kissed her cheek.

"It's what I do," she said. "Are we having salmon for dinner?"

"Indeed. How would you like me to fix it?"

"Brushed with dill and butter, please, Julian."

"Grilled?"

"Yes, that sounds lovely."

"Father, you look like a plum. Do you want some salmon, too?"

"She ... she ..." Walter tried to unclench his jaw, then grabbed his cane and stomped down the stairs and across the garden to the beach.

"I'll take that as a yes." Julian turned to his mother. "What did you say?"

"I told him I'm dying. Which you both already know." She smiled up into his brown eyes. "You will marry that girl soon, won't you?"

He squatted next to her and took her hand. "You *know* I will. But that isn't why he was so upset."

"No," she sighed. "I told him something I probably shouldn't have. I probably shouldn't tell you, either. I hope you get married soon."

"Yes, so you've said, even though you've also told me that we will."

She touched his broad cheek. "Seeing the future and being sure it will come to pass do not always go together. Especially when one's emotions are involved. The observer influences what she observes, and not always for the better."

"Yes, Mother," he said. "Come to the kitchen and tell me how much dill to use." He stood and held his hand out to her. She took it and stood, slowly and with a grimace of pain. "Shall I make you some of your tea?"

"Yes, please."

The kitchen was made of split pine, as was the furniture. It had been the first room they had built and was still her favorite. Walter had done almost all the work by himself. Ellen had spent most of

her time establishing the garden, while
Julian fished and hunted small game to
sustain them. It had been hard, and
lonely for Julian. Ellen had *seen* that
more people would join them, but she had
not seen any particulars. She had been
optimistic, but not sure, that there would
be a wife for Julian. She was still
optimistic, but not sure, that there would
be some with the genetic trait which
resulted in powers. It had always been a
fickle and unpredictable occurrence in
their far northern part of the world.

As Julian settled her at the kitchen
table, Ellen said, "He will be tempted to
look into the past. All the time." She
rubbed the worn wooden surface, scarred
from years of hard use.

"Yes, I know." He put the kettle on and
got out her favorite mug.

"You must not let him."

"Yes, I know."

She scowled up at him. "You know, for
the first time I understand what your
father means when he says I'm too
agreeable."

"That's good!" he exclaimed, falsely
hearty. "A real breakthrough in your
relationship."

"I don't appreciate this new sarcasm, either." She rubbed her aching hands.

"Do you want an extra teaspoon of willow bark?"

"Yes." He put the mug in front of her, and she sat back and sipped her tea, remembering. She and Walter had come here when Julian was thirteen, and they had been alone then. She had enjoyed that, the solitude. Seeing the future for three was much easier than seeing it for a village.

"Feel better?" asked Julian after a bit. He had cleaned the fish and was slicing it. She admired the sure movements of his big, brown hands. She had always hoped her vision of only one child would turn out to be untrue. "Mother?" Julian turned around.

"Yes. Yes, I am. Just remembering." The others had trickled into this valley, settled here on the shore of their little, landlocked lake. Walter was right. Julian had been much happier when Penny had arrived with her little sister.

Julian smiled. "That's Dad's job."

"Yes. I used to be a little jealous of that."

Julian put down his filet knife and washed his hands. "Jealous? Of Dad? Why?"

"Of seeing the past. So much more comfortable than seeing the future."

"But not as useful." He drizzled melted butter with lemon across the filets.

She shook her head. "That depends on the circumstances. Your father still has a part to play." Julian glanced at her, surprised. "At any rate," she continued, "people often enjoy remembering the past. They don't really want to know the future. They think they do, but they don't. Even good visions seldom turn out to be what you think they'll be."

Julian sprinkled dill on the salmon. "Enough?"

"More."

He smiled. "I better plant more dill." He crumbled and sprinkled the herb, put the salmon in the oven, and sat down at the table beside her. "I'm pretty sure Dad's been jealous of you."

"I know. Are you sorry you weren't gifted, Julian? You were angry about it when you were young. Then, when you were about twenty, you told me you were glad your life wasn't complicated by, I think you called it, 'hocus pocus.' How do you feel these days?"

"I feel I have enough to take care of with a regular life, and I don't know how you ever managed to balance your sight with everything else."

"I don't either."

They heard voices outside. "That sounds like Penny," said Julian, surprised. "And Maria."

"I don't think there's enough salmon for five. You'd better make some pilaf."

Walter entered, looking much happier than he had thirty minutes before. "I found treasure." He ushered in the two young women, both stocky, dark-haired, and round-cheeked. The elder went immediately to Julian and kissed him.

The younger went to Ellen and examined her carefully. "How are you?" she asked, her tone much older than her eleven years.

Penny turned in Julian's arms and said, "Maria insisted we come. I'm sorry to intrude so close to dinner."

"You know you're always welcome," said Julian. "Help me make some pilaf and join us in eating it."

Ellen faced the serious child with an equally intent gaze. "I am fine, Maria. Are you well?" Wisps of fine, black hair obscured the little girl's brow. Ellen brushed them back, gently smoothing out the furrows. "Did you *see* something, sweetheart?" Her quiet question seeped out into the room, a ripple of change.

Walter straightened up with an involuntary, "No." Ellen made a shushing gesture towards him.

Maria's chin trembled. "I saw you sick. I saw you — gone."

Walter sat down heavily. Julian, who had been checking the fish, turned around, blinking steam out of his eyes. Penny put a hand to her chest and murmured, "Ohhh."

"It's all right, Maria," said Ellen calmly. "I know all about it. It's all right." Maria sobbed and threw her arms around Ellen, who hugged her tightly, suppressing a grimace of pain as the child squeezed her. "Shh, shh, shh. Shh, shh, shh."

Ellen refused to discuss it until everyone had eaten. She ate very little these days herself but refused to see freshly grilled salmon sit untouched. The pilaf never happened, but they made do with leftover cornbread and salad. Ellen sipped her tea and prayed for strength.

"Now can we talk?" Walter pushed his plate away. "Did you *see* this, Ellen? Couldn't you have warned us that Maria would develop the sight?"

"You know I don't see everything. I can't demand it." Ellen turned to Maria. "This is a difficult thing that you have been called to do. I wish I could say different words to you. I wish I could promise to always be here to help you through." She shook her head. "I cannot."

"Do I have a choice?" whispered Maria. Her eyes were the color of the split pine walls.

"No. The visions will come. But you will have guidance in how to deal with them."

"And who will be doing that?" demanded Walter.

Ellen smiled, almost laughed. "You will." She looked around the table. "You all will."

Julian and Penny were holding hands, Penny's eyes shining with tears. "How, Ellen? How can I possibly help her with this?"

"Well, you've made a good start by falling in love with my son. He has a lifetime of watching me process visions."

Julian tilted his head inquiringly and opened his mouth.

"Don't be ridiculous, Ellen," burst out Walter. "Watching isn't enough."

Ellen turned and lifted one hand to touch his cheek. "I know how hard all of this is for you. But you must be strong and courageous. For Maria."

Walter glanced at the child and lowered his eyes. "I just don't understand," he muttered.

"I think Mom can explain things, Dad." Julian rolled his eyes. "She's just doing it in her own good time, as usual." He glanced around. "That was supposed to make you all smile."

Penny tried to smile at him. "Maybe... maybe Maria should go out and say hello to the goats for a few minutes," she suggested.

Maria looked at her sister, torn, desperate to escape all this tension, but also desperate to know.

"Let us figure things out, chick, then we'll talk, okay?" said Penny gently.

Maria's face lightened. "Okay." She touched Ellen's arm gently. "You'll be okay?"

"Oh, yes, sweetheart, I'll be right here for a while yet."

Maria stood up, hugged Ellen again, and rushed out the back door.

The adults drew breath. Penny sobbed, Walter cursed. Julian hugged his fiancee and said, "Am I right in assuming that Dad is going to be remembering a lot over the next few days?"

Ellen smiled. "Are you sure you don't have the sight?"

"Ellen, please." Walter closed his eyes. "When you foresaw the flooding, it was so —" he searched for words "— so hard to cope. How are the three of us going to be able to help a child like Maria if she should have a vision as difficult as — as that was — without you?"

"You'll have my memories, Walter. You and I are going to make sure you have everything you need."

They began the next morning, while they were still in bed. Walter opened a window into the past, and she helped him find the memories she believed would help Maria. He had not often been called to use his gift in this way; he had to "mark" the remembrances so that he would be able to find them again, when they were needed. After her death.

They began with Ellen's earliest recollections of her own first visions. Her parents had found a seer to help her understand and develop her gift. There had been hundreds of people in the community they had grown up in, and several seers. Their warnings about the crisis to come had not been appreciated. When the sea level began to rise, and the visionaries told people they would have to give up their homes and their saltwater lives, some had turned on the seers. Walter and Ellen and their young son had fled from the violence of their panicked neighbors.

In this new little village, which now homed fewer than a hundred people, Ellen and Walter had been the only gifted ones. Until now.

After breakfast, they continued their work. "You know," said Ellen, "there may be another child out there. One with your gift. There's never been any predicting it. Even for those with the sight."

They were sitting on the porch again, watching their son working in the garden. He was harvesting for a feast. The wedding date had been brought forward.

Ellen had told them it needed to be, if she were to attend.

Walter grunted. "Let me get this one sorted first." He pulled his chair closer to hers and swiped at the air. "Here's when you were fifteen, and you *saw* your grandmother's death. I was with you that day. You cried a lot. I was only twelve, and I didn't know what to do."

Ellen smiled. "You did fine. You took me to Megan, which was just what I needed."

"Yes, see, that's what I mean. We don't have a Megan to take Maria to. We won't have you." His voice cracked.

"Yes, you will, Walter. You'll be able to take Maria to Megan. She'll get a vision of Megan, so she'll hear exactly what I heard. You and Julian and Penny just need to provide the physical part. Hug her and kiss her and tell her everything will be fine."

"Everything won't be fine."

"Yes, it will. It may take a while, but it will."

"You're an infernal optimist."

"A cockeyed optimist!" she sang, with only a slight tremor in her voice, "I'm only a cockeyed optimist, immature and incurably green!"

They didn't have movies anymore, but sometimes Walter opened a window to the past and played one for her. ("A blasted parlor trick," he called it.)

"You've never been immature," he said. "Not even when you were fifteen."

"I just didn't seem so to you, because three years younger is such a lot in teen years."

Walter sighed and marked the memory. "What comes next?"

Ellen's eyes sparkled mischievously. "I foresaw our first night together."

"But didn't tell me about it."

"Well, not then. How could I? You were just fourteen, and I was a very sophisticated seventeen. I went straight to Megan and begged her to tell me the future could be changed."

He paused in opening the window to this memory and said, "You never told me that part."

"No?" She closed her eyes. "Well, it was a bit much, you know. Walter, I think you and Julian and Penny should review these memories together — before they are needed. I think it will help you to help Maria if you are all forewarned about how it may go."

"And what if it doesn't go this way?"

"All the more reason to be forewarned. Oh, Walter, it will be close enough. Young women mature along a fairly predictable timeline. Megan managed."

"Megan had the sight!" Walter pounded his fist on the arm of his chair. His raised voice caused his son to look up from his work in the garden.

Ellen groaned and seemed to shrink in her chair. "Walter, what can I say? This is the best I can do."

He slid out of his chair and knelt at her feet. "I'm sorry," he whispered. "I'm sorry. I'm just so frightened, Ellie."

She stroked his white hair, still so thick and soft. "I know. But Walter, you're so much stronger than you think you are. There's never been a time when you weren't able to do what was needed."

In bed that night, he held her gently. "Tell me," he said slowly.

"Yes?"

"Tell me why you begged Megan to change the future. I mean, I saw what you said to her, but still —" She shook in his arms. "Are you laughing?" he demanded.

"Yes. I'm sorry." She kissed his chest. "I had never had sex, Walter. I had never even kissed a boy."

"Well, I should hope not. Whom would you kiss?"

Silence.

"You didn't kiss —"

"I am not going to discuss with you who I did or did not kiss before we were married." She was shaking with laughter again. "Not at this stage of my life. My point is, that seeing the experience of an orgasm with a boy who was, to me at that time, a snotty fourteen-year-old, was an existential shock. I panicked. And Megan helped me, as always, and she will help Maria, too, if such a thing should happen to her."

"Oh," said Walter with a groan. "Oh, Ellie, I really, really can't handle this."

"Yes, you can."

"No, no, I can't."

"Yes, yes, you can." She tickled him and he jerked. "If it makes you feel any better, I've seen you dead before Maria is seventeen. That's why you need to be sure to share all the remembrances with Julian and Penny."

He stared into the darkness. "No, no, I don't believe that makes me feel any better." His arms tightened gently around her. "But... it doesn't make me feel any worse, either." He sounded surprised.

"No raging?"

"No raging."

"Hogwash." Her voice smiled in the dark. "You'll rage. When I see you again, I'll know you immediately, because your spirit will be plum-colored."

"Have you *seen* that?"

"No." She shook her head, her wispy hair brushing his chest. "But I can depend on you, Walter. In all the chaos we've endured, I've always known you would be there for me, raging on my behalf."

He smiled. "Well. I can handle that."

Susan McDonough-Wachtman's story "I Will Go Gently" was published in Metaphorosis on Friday, 14 December 2018.

About the story

I was inspired to write "I Will Go Gently" by a dream. I woke up one morning with the vision of an old couple on a porch, arguing amicably about something — the way my parents used to. The interesting and different aspect about this couple was that, unlike my parents, she could see the future, and he could look into the past. I didn't know where they'd come from or how their "gifts" affected their lives. I discovered their story as I wrote. I worked in my worry about global warming, my pain from the slow death of my mother, my hope for the future of my children. It was easy to see how the woman's gift could be worked into a story of global warming, but it was a bit of a challenge to see how the man's gift could be made integral to the plot. Having the story set in the far north seemed logical to me. If anyone was going to foresee the need to move inland and could find a new setting for a future community, I thought it would be the natives of northern Canada. Or perhaps I should say it will be. Because in spite of everything, I foresee a future for the human race which involves a better system than the one we have now.

A question for the author

Q: Do you have a garden? Have you ever grown your own food?

A: I have often gardened, although I have never been a great success. Moving every few years, raising kids, and teaching school made it hard to find the time and energy. We got lucky a few times. We moved into one house in Western Oregon with well-established and highly productive raspberries. When the kids were young, we planted peas and beans in Western Washington and learned to battle slugs every morning. Now that I have an empty nest, we are living in my husband's family home and benefit from well-established blueberry bushes. We compete with the birds for those. I am still trying to grow peas and beans, but now have to keep away the deer and wild rabbits. We also grew a wide variety of squash this year. My husband is a wonderful cook and we've been enjoying baked squash and squash soup.

About the author

Susan McDonough-Wachtman has been a burger tosser, customer service rep, ad taker, curriculum developer, parent, reader, kayaker, gardener, and high school teacher. She lives in the Pacific Northwest with one cat and one husband.

susanmcdonoughwachtman.wordpress.com, @SusanMcdW

Family Tree

Lindsey Duncan

"Halett," Rithshara called out of her dressing chamber, "where is my youngest son?" She pondered the crimson headdress versus the black, and decided on the former, which didn't pinch. There was no reason menace couldn't be comfortable.

"Serving his unjust punishment in the underworld," Halett replied. The dark, wiry man with the odd eyes — one brown, one blue — was clever, but occasionally, he tried too hard.

She frowned. "My youngest living son, Halett. He was supposed to accompany me on the day's diversions."

"I will find him."

Thanks to a bath of eternal youth, Rithshara did not look anything close to her hundred and fifty years, but after her sixth husband's untimely assassination — this time, it had not been her doing — she had retired and handed the reins to her daughter Glivren. That was four years ago; she now had the distinction of being history's only recorded Evil Overmother, with the luxury to pursue her hobbies of esoteric execution methods, dream torture, and mountain-climbing.

The titian-haired sorceress arrayed herself on her resting couch with a sigh. Her oldest son had set himself up as a minor god. Her second son had made a deal with demons to open a gateway to other worlds and sought a paradise worth the plucking. Both her daughters were skilled in the dark arts. Then there was Othri.

"Empress?"

She sat up. "Where is my son?"

"Gone. Left the city." Halett's words were clipped.

Rithshara had abandoned the practice of executing the messenger because it was hard on personnel, but it was tempting to revert. Save that it was Halett, who was too valuable to lose. She had almost gotten out of the habit of watching her back around him. Almost. "You looked everywhere? So quickly?"

"I didn't have to. He left a note."

Halett minced into the room, keeping up a brave face. She plucked the note from his hand.

Dear Mother, it began. *I am afraid I have reached a point where I must follow my conscience.*

That was his problem right there. Any member of his family could have helped him remove the pesky thing. He had always been a puzzle to her, befriending servants and hostages. Granted, the latter had come in handy once or twice …

She read on. *I am leaving the city and the empire to devote myself as a priest to the Gods of Light. May you and our family one day wake to the error of your ways.*

Truth Sings, Othri

Rithshara rose in a dramatic swirl of skirts. "Halett? We have work to do."

In his nineteen years, Othri had grown resigned to wild rides on the back of spiny demons, or gut-wrenching teleportation that left one with a deep-seated need for chicken soup. He found he enjoyed walking.

Even though this had been the Ash Forest for over a century, traces of the Firegreen still surfaced. Vine-roses trellised up the withered trees, a trickle of water bubbled across a dry riverbed, and songbirds mocked the vultures and demon-birds who made this place their home. The old had not been completely smothered, and Othri felt its tranquility. He closed his eyes and breathed.

He tripped over a root.

"Good grief." He picked himself up out of the mud. "Well, now I suppose I have a disguise." He had toyed with dyeing his fox-red hair, but his family had easier ways to find him if they wished. He had always been a disappointment; he hoped they wouldn't miss him.

"That's a terrible disguise."

His head whipped about, but he saw no one. Despite the voice's raspy, thorny quality, he was sure the speaker was female.

"I'm sorry," he said, "is someone there?"

"More or less." She walked out of a tree trunk as if it were a doorway, a stout, brawny woman with skin the same color as the withered leaves. Grey moss hair twined down her back and shoulders and fused with both. Its color notwithstanding, she looked about his age.

Othri stared. It did not take years of eldritch training to identify a forest spirit, bound to the forest and its guardianship, but he had expected something more ethereal, more exotic.

She planted her hands on her hips. "What?"

There was no way to tactfully put words to his confusion. "Are you …"

She strode closer without seeming to move her feet. He did a surreptitious check: she did indeed have feet. "Kebra. I'm the spirit of the Ash Forest."

"Othri. I'm nobody."

"That's obviously not true," she said, "since you're standing here talking to me. Covered in mud."

"Well, I'm somebody," he amended, "but nobody important."

She frowned and studied him; he felt as if his soul were being raked through underbrush. "I doubt that, but I don't care as long as you don't hurt my forest."

"I'm not here to harm anyone," he said. He had learned young that appearances were misleading, that great beauty could hide great evil, but he had never heard anything about the other way around. Kebra was far from ugly, but she had a solid strength he had not expected. "So you are the mistress of the Firegreen?"

"No, I'm the mistress of the Ash Forest. I came into being after the plague destroyed the old trees and their ever-branches stopped burning. What became of the spirit before me, I have no idea. I'm the forest as it is now: a survivor." Kebra spoke in a matter of fact tone, but thunderstorm shadow flickered in her eyes. "It's all I am and know."

"I'm honored to meet you," he said.

She snorted, turning away. "Why have you come to my forest?"

"I'm just passing through. I'm headed to the Silver City."

"How cosmopolitan of you," she said. "What are you going to do there?"

"I intend to become a novice in the order of Thiorsan," he said, "and some day, a priest. If the god deems me worthy."

"So you're going to sit in marble halls, play endless lullabies, and meditate on the purpose of existence until you can't feel your toes," Kebra said. "Sounds like a great way to live your life."

Her sarcasm was thicker than the mud on his pants. He ignored it. "I hope so. It will be a nice change."

She stared. "From what?"

As the first answer that came to mind was "demon summoning," and the second was "world domination," he hesitated. His mother had created the Ash Forest in her early days, so he knew what topics to avoid. "I've had a rough life," he said, awkward. He had always felt comfortable talking to people, even mad sorcerers and extraplanar beings, but Kebra turned his words upside down.

"You sure don't look like it," she said. "Good luck, then. If Thiorsan deigns to materialize for you, tell him I said hello." She turned away.

"Wait!" he said. "Am I going the right ..." He stopped as she stepped into the tree trunk and disappeared.

He sighed, then gathered up his optimism and his compass. He headed onwards, unable to resist whistling a hymn. His new life was near, and he had met a forest spirit. It was a good day.

Rithshara stood before her scrying pool, lacquered obsidian nails arrayed on the bone rim. It had once been some the skull of great beast called a dinosaur, a gift from her late third husband — the bones, not the beast.

"Empress?" When she waved him in, Halett continued, "I've given your regrets to your daughter in regards to today's presentation of slaves."

Rithshara had forgotten the commitment in the unnecessary drama. She found herself grateful for Halett's foresight — not for the first time. "And you didn't tell her why?"

"Of course not." Beneath his servility, Halett seemed indignant.

"Good." She traced one fingernail across the murky surface, spelling out her enchantment in invisible calligraphy. "Othri," she breathed to the pool. "Show me my son."

The pool's surface quivered and cleared, depicting a small, rotund toddler with scarlet curls. He played under a thorn tree with a puppy he'd somehow found — not a proper hellhound, but a scruffy moppet. She remembered that day — an early warning sign of his softness.

Rithshara sighed. "Show me my son today," she amended.

The pool's surface rippled again, and an image formed of disheveled Othri tramping through a forest.

"That's the Ash Forest," Halett said.

Natural outings were not Rithshara's idea of a vacation, and she had not set foot under the Forest's bowers for decades. "So it is," she said. "And not far from the border. How in the world is he traveling, by horse?"

Halett leaned over the bowl. "By foot. Horses will not tolerate the Ash Forest."

Rithshara laughed. "Walking? Now I've heard everything."

"It is, if nothing else, a reliable method of transportation."

She wasn't sure whether to be impressed by her son's determination or annoyed by his stupidity. "He might have stolen one of Glivren's brooms, at least."

"I expect he didn't want to give you any reason to chase him."

"As if I would abandon my darling boy."

"Children usually don't know their parents that well," Halett observed. When she shot him a look, he added, "I've a daughter, Empress. She's nine."

"Well," Rithshara murmured. Halett had been a trusted hand for years, yet she never would have guessed. She'd have to pay more attention to him in the future. "In any event, this makes things simple. I shall bring him back promptly."

Halett cleared his throat. "If I may make another suggestion?"

He had to be aware that for lesser minions, those were frequently last words. "Continue."

"If you go to retrieve him yourself, it will make too big a show," he said. "This thing needs to be done quietly, to match his disgrace. I would recommend sending an ice dragoneer."

She considered. Halett was right: the last thing she wanted was to provide fodder for gossip. An Evil Overmother had her tyrannical image to maintain.

"Very well," she said. "Send the dragoneer."

Othri had never walked this far in his life, and the novelty had worn off. He plopped down on a stump and eased his boots off to massage his feet.

"I suppose it builds character," he said.

The sudden chill in the air surprised him. Though the fire trees had long since burned out, lingering embers flickered in their trunks, and Othri had grown used to their warmth. In summer, it might have been stifling, but on this early spring day, the heat had served as a comforting cocoon ... until now.

In the distance, a harpy shrilled over her meal. Otherwise, the forest was still. Wary, he slid off the stump, crouching and wishing he still had his boots on. The canopy rustled.

He dove under the nearest bush as a blast of icy breath seared through the clearing. It froze stump, ground, and boots.

Ice dragon! He rolled to one side, peering up through the maze of hoary leaves. The dragon's wings flashed; he caught just enough glimpse to see the saddle and rider.

He continued rolling, crawling elbows and knees into deeper underbrush. His heart throbbed in anxiety, making it difficult to breathe. He was a traitor to his family and might be treated as such.

Something snagged his pack, and he resisted the urge to plead for his life. He grimaced and yanked, but the crackling of branches told him his adversary was only a thorn-bush.

The sound caught the attention of the dragon. It wheeled with a cry like shattering ice. Othri winced and tried to crawl faster. He debated lurching to his feet to sprint, but once upright, he would be exposed and barefoot.

Arctic blasts poured around him. The nearby trees frosted over, lacquered in hues of unnatural blue. The sweat froze on his back, but the ground beneath him was undisturbed. It meant he wasn't in the epicenter. The dragoneer didn't know where he was ... yet. He breathed out cautiously, watching it fog, and lifted his head to peer through the icicle trees.

The dragon's powerful wingbeats vibrated the air. Twigs and ice-coated leaves shattered. The dragon circled overhead ... retreating? He dared to hope the rider might have given up.

Othri flinched down as the dragon swept back overhead, a second layer of ice frosting over the first. So much for hiding. He tucked his legs beneath him, ready to leap — stagger — to his feet.

The nearest trees caught flame, blazing skywards in sunset coruscation. He gasped at the beauty.

"Are you going to stand there and stare, or are you coming?" Kebra's voice demanded.

Othri almost toppled searching for her. Her face gleamed in the fire. "How do I ..."

"Just plunge into the flame," she said, impatient.

It occurred to him, through force of habit, that this would be a very easy way to kill him, but he wanted to trust her. He stumbled upright and charged the tree.

Heat flared around him, but did not burn. Bark rasped across his skin, yet the tree was soft, a cushion of feathers. He tumbled through into a clearing.

Kebra stood before him, arms crossed. "You have ice dragons chasing you," she said, "so you're obviously not nobody. Who are you?"

There seemed to be nothing for it. "I'm the son of Overmother Rithshara," he said.

Moving like a gale, she slapped him. "You idiot!"

This had happened so many times, he had a conditioned response. "Yes, I am. Terribly sorry."

Kebra stared. "You ... what?" Recovering, she went on, "You really thought you could just walk away? That they wouldn't follow you?"

"I honestly didn't think they'd care," he said.

She snorted. "Well, thanks for not thinking, because now my forest is a target."

He swallowed. "I'm sorry. I'll leave as soon as I can, I promise."

"And when you get to the Silver City, is that really what you're going to do? Live a cloistered life in the service of priesthood?"

Othri had borne her indignation as the rightful product of her forest coming under attack, but now he felt he had to defend himself. "I've lived a life full of black magic and ambition. Don't you think I want to get as far away from that as possible?"

"So travel the world," she said. "Visit the Great Library of Tareish. Roam the Golden Dunes. Dance in festivals in every city. Dine in taverns where they don't speak your language. Learn a musical instrument they've never heard of in the Empire. It's what I'd do."

She was right: there was a greater world, but he doubted he was equipped for it. The priesthood was safe, assured shelter from the chaos of the Empire. "So why don't you?"

She flinched. "I can't. I'm trapped within the bounds of the trees. I can only see where the Ash Forest's seeds have flown, but having adapted to this waste," she raked a hand around her, "they don't grow well anywhere else. They have to be planted deep in ash."

"I'm sorry," he said, regretting the question. "I could take a sapling with me when I leave."

"So all I would get to see is the halls of Thiorsan?" she countered.

"Isn't that better than no halls?"

She turned away, drifting between the trees. By now, he was certain her feet didn't move. "I guess."

"It's the least I can do," he said, "after I've put you out."

She paused, glaring over her shoulder. "Are you going to move? The sooner you leave, the faster things will go back to normal."

"Can't we just step through a tree again and be at the edge of the forest?"

"I can," she answered, "you can't. It takes a lot out of me to move a mortal."

Othri scampered after, wincing as a broken branch scraped his foot. "You don't have to look out for me."

"Yes," she said, "I do." And despite his polite questions and bright remarks about their surroundings, she said nothing else for some time. He was used to being able to get through to people, but Kebra was as bleak as the forest she guarded.

"What do you mean, you think you had him? Where is he?" Rithshara glared up from her velvet couch.

"Well ..." the dragoneer faltered. "My mount had his scent and we had frozen down the area, when a bank of trees erupted into flames. When the smoke cleared, we had lost his aroma. We circled for over an hour, but couldn't pick up another trace."

Rithshara wondered what her youngest son smelled like: violets and timidity? "You are dismissed," she said. The dragoneer tripped over the rug in his haste to absent himself. "You warned him to expect the worst, didn't you, Halett?"

He shrugged. "I may have done, Empress."

She found herself impressed again. When had she come to rely upon him? Pity her son didn't have the same instincts. Othri had a knack for people, but it was the wrong one. "A worthy thought. Perhaps I should have ... no." Disappearing dragoneers would doubtless draw dubious attention to this diversion of hers. "The spirit of the forest has involved herself, Halett."

"How do you know it's a woman?"

"Divine division of labor," she said. "Females take rivers and forests; males take oceans and mountains. It's aggravatingly sexist."

"What do we do now?"

"There's nothing else to be done: I shall have to go myself. You will accompany me." Rithshara sighed. "I hope it won't take much to bring the boy to his senses."

"I don't see how it could," Halett said. "The advantages he has by being under your wing are tremendous."

Rithshara nodded absently, accepting that. Learning to flatter was a basic skill of underlings. She expected it from Halett as a matter of course. She rose and moved to her bookshelf. She skimmed tomes bound variously with skin, bone and fruitcake, pulling one out. "I'm opening a portal as close to his current location as possible. I expect you will defend me from the forest, if necessary."

Due to an abundance of heroes who thought they could topple the Empire, the imperial armory had acquired a stock of magical weapons. These had been distributed to top officers, and Halett carried one of sufficient strength to cut through whatever enchantments the forest had to offer.

"My arm is at your service, Empress," he said.

She paused, arching an eyebrow. "And the rest of you, I should hope."

"Even my freckles."

"You don't have freckles."

He cleared his throat pointedly.

She laid the book out on her ritual stand. To an outsider, the ancient language would have sounded like a cross between gargling and a madrigal.

The portal flared into existence, white and oozing. She took Halett's extended arm and stepped through.

On the other side, she inhaled. Ah, the Ash Forest ... a monument to the achievements of her youth. She drank in the decay and darkness, smiling as a spectre flitted overhead.

Othri was somewhere here, and every moment closer to disappearing. She murmured another spell, her voice growing to eldritch strength. She whooped, her voice powering through the trees. It reflected back to her, mapping out what lay beyond.

A counter-melody interrupted, discordance that made it impossible to pick up the echoes. She scowled.

Halett rubbed his ears. "Empress?"

"The spirit of the forest is interfering with my powers." She pursed her lips. "Well. I can take care of that."

"Better than Thiorsan's eunuch-mangled yowling, isn't it?" Kebra asked.

"It is certainly different," Othri said, trying to be tactful. The pain in his feet was distracting, but that was no cause to be surly.

"I've blocked your mother's seeking spell, but she'll come up with something else soon. We need to move." She put action to words, zipping through the trees without regards to human locomotion.

"Or she'll hurt your forest," Othri murmured.

She whipped about to face him, vine tendril tresses moving in sync. "That's a chance I'm willing to take."

"I'm not," he said firmly. Fear flowed up in him, but what would his new life be if he paved the way with blood? Or whatever vital fluid ran through the veins of a forest spirit.

Kebra folded her arms, expression cross. "So you're going to go back. Just like that."

"If I have to." He would only be giving up a change of scenery, after all. Perhaps Kebra's harping had some ring of truth, and Thiorsan's halls, as superior as they were to his family's palace, might eventually become familiar and even boring. "Who did she bring with her?"

Her eyes unfocused. "Just one man — scrawny sort with mismatched eyes."

"Halett," he said. He remembered the man, a trusted but invisible part of the imperial entourage. At times, he had envied Halett his competence in their world of conspiracies. His brain, scampering about in search of some other solution, almost tripped over an idea. "I need to talk to him."

"Do you really think this is going to be solved by talking?"

"Just this once," he replied, "it might be."

Kebra heaved a gusty sigh. "She's already sent him to scout the area, probably so he doesn't see whatever mysterious feminine ritual she's about to enact."

"I always thought that was a metaphor for something," Othri said.

"Do you think I'd tell you if it was? All I have to do is ask the forest to close in around him."

"Let's do it."

She led him through the forest, the trees twisting and pirouetting out of her way. He watched in fascination as the patterns became a corridor, impenetrable on either side. Kebra gestured; he followed, keeping his limbs close. He was not so sure the trees would not snap at him in passing.

Othri heard Halett first, crunching through the underbrush and cursing. The trees shifted, and he stumbled into view.

"Othri!" Halett jerked upright. "What kind of mad chase is this?"

"One you started, as far as I can tell," Kebra said.

Halett's eyes narrowed, assessing her. "Milady," he said, frosty in his absolute politeness. "This is not your fight. It's time he went home."

"I'm afraid I'm not going home, Halett," Othri said.

Halett slid a hand to his sword hilt. "I'm afraid you are."

"That's odd, neither of you looks afraid," Kebra said. Othri was grateful for the words, for he certainly felt the fear. Not so much of Halett, though the man was formidable; he was afraid what his mother would do, and how the forest — and Kebra — would be affected.

"I don't belong there," Othri said. "I'm just going to be a continuing disappointment to my mother until she decides to get rid of me permanently."

"That's her luxury," Halett countered, "but not necessarily. You seem smart and adaptable, Othri. You could find a way to follow the family line."

"You have more faith in me than I do. Maybe you're right, but that's not who I want to be. And do you really want me there, Halett?" he asked. "Or would you rather her attention go to someone more deserving?"

Halett stiffened in surprise. "It's not my place to decide who is worthy and who is not."

"You would make a better son than I would," Othri said. "If I had my way, you'd just take my place."

Halett opened his mouth, shut it. Othri pressed on. "I want her to let me go."

"So you can go off and do nothing in particular," Kebra said, sotto voce, possibly to the vines. The words stung; he told himself she wasn't right, but wasn't sure he believed it.

"She won't," Halett said. "She can't allow the world to see her son betray her."

The loyalty in Halett's voice both impressed and relieved Othri. He knew he could settle any doubts on that count. "I know. And I have an idea."

The ritual Rithshara intended would be swift and irrevocable, which was why it took so long: it had been designed to give the spellcaster time for second thoughts. For her, the delay was merely annoying. Second thoughts were something that happened to other people.

She glanced about the mire-laden clearing with some irritation. Why had Halett not returned? If the forest spirit had somehow overcome such a trusted lieutenant, she would feel Rithshara's wrath, and not simply because the Overmother had an image to maintain. As her attention shifted, she realized the forest thrummed.

The trees parted, revealing the trio of Halett, Othri — he was barefoot, she noted with bemusement — and a wood-knotted woman who must be the forest spirit.

"Ah," Rithshara said, "it all makes sense now. This is about a woman."

Othri blinked owlishly. "What? No, it isn't about Kebra."

"She doesn't seem like his type," Halett said.

"What about my type?" the spirit asked.

"I wouldn't presume to guess."

Kebra turned to Othri. "Will you please get these people out of my forest?"

Up until this point, Rithshara had watched with bemused tolerance. "I would be careful how you address 'these people,' " she said, "seeing as some of us are responsible for your very existence. I trust you have come to surrender yourself?"

"I haven't," Othri said.

"Then I have no other recourse but to force you." She dashed away the ritual trappings with a swipe of her sleeve, grasping the dagger. A touch of blade against her skin summoned blood and power. Her whispers sent it whirling out, spiraling into rusty tentacles. They surged for Othri. "It's for your own good."

Halett stepped between them. "No." He brought the armory blade around in a theatrical arc, slashing through the air and the spell.

"What is the meaning of this?" she demanded.

"Hear him out."

She narrowed her eyes in displeasure and repeated the spell, punching out the words. The tentacles doubled and tripled, evading Halett's impressive technique. One set of bands coiled around Kebra, restraining the spirit. The rest converged on Othri.

They stopped.

The darkness hovered at the threshold of his body, refusing to bind him. Clearly confused, he wobbled back. In the contrast presented by her sorcery, Rithshara saw why. Purity. The boy was too good, in all the wrong ways.

"We both know I won't live up to the family legacy," Othri said, regaining his calm. "In the end, I'm only going to embarrass you."

"We are an empire and a bloodline," Rithshara said, "but most important of all, we are a family. We must present a united face to the world." She reached for a maternal tool more powerful than sorcery: the guilt trip. "Do you want to put your siblings in danger?"

"I don't think anything I could do would put my siblings in danger," he said, "but I wasn't made for this kind of life. Halett, on the other hand, is ideally suited. He is quick, clever and strong. Tell the world we were switched at birth. He is your true son, and I ... am nobody."

Rithshara stared, astonished beyond dignity. "Are you truly suggesting ..."

"You're right," he said, "that your son should be menacing and cunning. Of course you understand that can't be me."

She hesitated, knocked off course by the fact he was agreeing with her. "You have the ability. It's in your blood."

"Maybe, but I don't want it. Isn't ambition better from someone obsessed with it?"

"Here now, let's not go that far," Halett murmured.

She shifted her attention to him. "I suppose you support this idea, Halett."

"Yes, Empress, I do think the idea is sound," he replied, "though you understand my personal bias."

Kebra snorted. "Personal bias."

If only Othri would apply that mindset to the family business. Rithshara contemplated Halett. Othri was correct there: she could not have designed a better heir.

Suspicion reared its head. She tightened the magic threads surrounding Kebra. "What is your role in this? If you have poisoned him against me, I will destroy you."

"No," Othri said, "you won't. She had nothing to do with my departure." Deliberately, he stepped to the spirit's side … and the tentacles around her receded, fleeing from him.

"I had no role in this until Othri tumbled into my territory," Kebra said, apparently unmoved by the threat. "The result doesn't affect me unless you decide to start destroying the forest … again."

Rithshara ignored the pointed addendum.

"But one thing I know," Kebra continued, "is life grows from the consequences we didn't intend. Otherwise, I wouldn't be here. You could drive yourself mad trying to stifle everything that branches out — or you could embrace it."

Rithshara regarded Othri's anxious, unassuming face, a visage that wouldn't hold guile or malice. He stood barefoot, mud-spattered, but straight as an arrow with determination, and so counter to everything the family stood for that her powers refused to touch him. With a pass of her hands, she released the spell.

"You understand," she said, "that you will never have the same chance for power, influence, and wealth? You know the riches you're giving up?"

"Yes," he said, "and that's all right by me."

"You understand you will not be able to command the peasants in your new home to obey your every whim?"

He blinked. "I figured I would look after my own whims."

She really had no idea what to make of him. "Very well," she said. "I will put the plan into action as soon as I return to the palace."

He heaved a gusty sigh. "Thank you, mother," he said. "I will miss you — and the rest of the family — but this is what I need to do."

"I will miss you, too," Rithshara said, "but it appears there's no dissuading you." She paused. There was something missing. Realizing what it was, she did the unthinkable.

She embraced him.

Othri held onto the hug. This goodbye was harder than the first, but the knowledge he was free — really free — filled him with possibility. He hadn't imagined he would be able to get them both to agree, but the right words had just seemed natural.

"Thank you," he said.

"This is all very touching," Kebra said, "but can we get the evil overlady —"

"Overmother," Rithshara corrected.

"Whatever," the spirit snapped. "Can we get her out of my forest, please?"

Othri snuck a sideways look at Halett and caught a glimpse of the man's smirk. He had no worries; Halett would be just fine.

"Just remember who made it your forest," Rithshara said.

"Oh, I remember, believe me."

Halett pulled Othri aside. He tensed, waiting for some dire threat, but also feeling an eerie confidence that he could talk his way out.

"Do you need boots," Halett said, droll, "or are you making some kind of point?"

"Definitely the former," Othri said, fervent.

It was a quick exchange. Othri wasn't about to complain when it turned out Halett's boots were too big. It seemed some kind of metaphor.

With an inordinately complex gesture, his mother opened the portal. She and Halett stepped through. Demon birds caroled in the trees as the light winked out.

It was Kebra's turn to breathe a sigh of relief. "I didn't expect that to work."

"Could I get a few dozen seeds from you, please?" Othri said.

She crossed her arms. "I don't want dozens of sprouts channeling me devotional hymns and pitiful prayers for hours on end. It will drive me crazy."

"How would you tell the difference?" he asked with a small smile.

She barked laughter. "Fair."

"I'm still going to the Silver City," he said, "but not to become a novice. I never thought I had any strengths: now I know I have at least one."

"You're good with people," she said, "considering you just got that bastion of evil to do something decent."

He nodded, finding confidence in her agreement. "I have the chance to go anywhere. It seems a shame to waste it."

"Right." Kebra turned her hand over. Seeds spilled between her fingers. He stretched out the bottom of his shirt to catch them, and transferred them to his pockets.

"I could," he said, "plant one in Thiorsan's courtyard —"

"Don't you dare," she snapped. She pivoted and flowed through the trees, vines and leaves bending to greet her passage. Othri watched her go, smiling. His first encounter outside the Empire hadn't gone so badly.

She paused, turned back, hands arrayed on hips. "Well? Are you coming?"

"Coming?" he echoed, puzzled.

"I'm escorting you to the edge of my forest," she said. "You've caused enough trouble today."

He grinned. "I'd welcome the company."

Talking, sometimes bickering, they crossed the Ash Forest together, with all the world beyond.

Lindsey Duncan's story "Family Tree" was published in Metaphorosis on Friday, 21 December 2018.

About the story

"Family Tree" started as a writing prompt. I belonged to an online speculative fiction writers' group who had weekly hour-long write-ins, called "Friday Night Writes," even though they weren't always on Fridays (and weren't even always at night). One writer would post a prompt, and everyone else would get down as much as they could in that hour, then share their pieces. It was always great fun. I don't remember what the prompt was for "Family Tree," but I suspect it had something to do with writing from a villain's point of view. I've done this in the past, but I must have been in a lighter mood, because my brain went in a tongue-in-cheek direction, considered a retired evil overlord — make that an evil overmother. The opening of "Family Tree" fell out from there, with Othri's letter kicking off the plot. That was as far as I got during the free-write. I came back to it later to build out the story. One of the first things I decided I needed was an ally for Othri, and that brought Kebra into the story:

not a willowy, timid forest sprite, but the kind of hardy creature that would spring from a ravaged forest. ... and, of course, that's how I came up with the title.

A question for the author

Q: How does writing speculative fiction affect your daily life (not as a writer but as a person)?

A: Being a speculative fiction writer means that life is rarely boring. I've always got some plot point to chew on, and the oddest details in life might inspire a story. I'm always asking, "What if?" and spinning thoughts from that. But it's also entertaining because (at least for me), it's fostered a tendency to take metaphor literally. You have no idea how disappointed I was to find out that "Entertaining Silverware" just sits there. I also find that writing speculative fiction makes me both more open-minded and more skeptical. Speculative fiction is about what-if, considering what could be true or become true, so it tends to break down the tendency to say, "This is impossible." On the other hand, when everything *could* be true in some world, I find I'm less inclined to proclaim (even to myself) that "this is so" in our world. My reaction to a theory or belief that sounds plausible is not so much to accept it as to acknowledge that it could make a good story.

About the author

Lindsey Duncan is a chef / pastry chef, professional Celtic harp performer and life-long writer. She feels that music and language are inextricably linked. She lives in Cincinnati, Ohio.

www.LindseyDuncan.com, @lindseycduncan

Cinders and Snow

Kathryn Yelinek

The prince was old before his time. Candlelight from ballroom chandeliers softened the gray in his hair. He whirled yet another eligible young lady through a minuet, his movements practiced and sure, but he limped, round-shouldered. He was not yet twenty-five.

"The hall looks so elegant," the lady simpered between steps. "Like a winter wonderland."

"My mother's idea." Roderick smiled because he should. "She knew a ball would melt the midwinter cold." The queen mother sat across the room, on the dais beside his older brother the king, and the new queen.

"So wise." The lady batted her lashes. They fell across her skin like shadows over snow. Despite the room's warmth, Roderick shivered.

This simpering lady was not for him. Nor were the scores of other ladies he had dutifully paraded around the dance floor. He wished his mother wouldn't push so hard; the only lady he wanted he could not have.

I must see you married, his mother had said as she planned the ball. *Your brother is still childless, though he is eight years wed.*

But no lady deserved to be tied to him. He was an ill-luck prince, destined to hurt those he loved. Not even a mother's hope could melt his winter.

The music stopped, and he escaped to a balcony. He sat on the marble bench, its chill seeping through his wool trousers. He stretched his left leg beside him, and the throbbing in his knee ebbed. He sighed in relief.

Fresh snow carpeted the gardens and reflected light from the palace windows, making the night gray and murky. The evergreen trees he'd nursed from saplings stood like islands amid the snowdrifts: a spruce, a fir, a juniper.

Music swelled inside the ballroom, the opening strains of a pavane. Dancers would be taking their places, two by two, but the prince remained on his bench, watching the spruce, the fir, the juniper. He wished he were another sort of man, more assertive, more confident, a man who could turn the steps of a dance to his own designs. But he was not. He was like those trees: solitary, buffeted, bending but not breaking, destined to weather life's storms alone.

He would not sleep after the ball. If he did, the nightmares would come.

In his dreams, he was seven again, ensconced behind a tapestry in the library. The wool scratched his arms, and the floorboards dug into his knees, but this was his favorite hiding place.

His tutor had given him a wondrous book: paintings of trees so lifelike he pressed his nose to the page. He inhaled not the sweetness of linden flowers but something better: the heady, dry aroma of Book.

He breathed in again and traced the needles of a larch with his finger. If his father the king caught him, he would get a caning. He should be in the yard with his brother, carrying weights, hefting bow and sword like a proper prince. He turned the page.

Footsteps crossed the library floor. Roderick tensed, rubbed the book's leather cover as a talisman. Maybe if he rubbed hard enough, the footsteps would pass by.

The tapestry was torn back. He stared into his father's scowling face. The king smelled of pepper, spices hot enough to make a man cry.

"Worthless boy!" The book went flying. "Didn't I tell you to go outside?"

He scrambled back, around the tapestry. A gaggle of advisors blocked his path to the door. They were tall men, broad, with legs like siege towers. Like his father, they were men who enjoyed ripping the branches off saplings.

He couldn't go out, so he went up. He scurried up a library ladder, the rungs slick against his fingers.

"Come down!" The king shook the ladder. Roderick clung to it, trembling. "No one wants a weakling for a prince."

The ladder stretched as high as the shelves, almost to the ceiling, far beyond the reach of the tallest man. Roderick locked slippery fingers around the next rung and took another desperate step up.

Ladders might be tall, but a father's control stretched farther.

The wood bucked beneath the boy. He missed a step, and the shelves with their books tilted around him.

"Roderick!" his mother screamed.

He slammed into the floor, his leg twisted under him. Pain exploded in brittle, white agony.

The pavane played on. Inside, all was light and warmth and dancing. Outside, his breath iced the air. The backs of his legs had gone numb. He wrapped his arms around his chest and sat still, unmoving.

At eighteen, he brought his sweetheart to his father and asked permission to marry. Ella was a solid, rosy-cheeked daughter of a northern duke, come to court to give a pair of deer hounds to the king. Ogres lived up north, it was said, and wolves stole infants from cradles. Against that, she assured him, the king was only a man.

That man was eating peppers again, chilies and jalapenos in a clay bowl at his elbow. He took a final bite, wiped his fingers on his trousers, and strode from his chair. As courtiers whispered, the king narrowed his eyes.

"You planning to slip a cuckoo into our nest, girl?"

"What?" Ella furrowed her brows.

Roderick clenched his fists. The king's breath was hot, fetid. "Father, please..."

The king slid his bejeweled hand over her stomach. She stiffened. The king slipped his hand inside her neckline, pinched.

"Father!" Roderick cried, even as Ella jerked back, her arms crossing over her breast.

"Must be you're carrying a cuckoo, girl. You're too pretty for my weakling son."

Ella shook her head. "Your Majesty, you're mistaken. I'm intact, and I love your son."

"You calling me a liar, girl?"

He was. The king was a liar, but who would name him so?

Ella lifted her chin. "Yes, Your Majesty."

The king's slap rang loud in the room. Roderick started forward, but his knee buckled. He fell, landing on hands and knees on the carpet. The court stood in shocked silence.

Ella pressed a hand to her reddening cheek. Blood welled between her fingers. The rest of her face was pale as snow.

"I am not a liar," the king said. "Say it."

Ella pressed her lips together.

"Say it!"

Roderick pushed himself painfully to his feet. "Just say it," he whispered. She did not need to be as meek as his brother's new wife, just pretend to be.

"I'm intact," Ella declared, "and I love your son."

The king's face burned scarlet. "Be gone, wench! Leave my lands, and never return."

Roderick gasped. Ella turned to him, her eyes pleading.

"Father, no—"

The king was already walking back to his chair. "Guards, see she is gone by sundown. If she refuses, put her forcibly in the streets."

"No!" Roderick gripped her hand. She wrapped her fingers around his arm, and he took courage from her strength. "I'll go with her," he announced.

The king rolled his eyes. He made a shooing motion with his fingers before selecting another pepper.

For one glorious moment, Roderick believed the king would let him go. He clasped Ella's hand, his heart as light as a leaf on the wind. Together they backed towards the door.

They took half a dozen steps before guards dragged them apart.

"Ella!" he cried, his arm wrenched behind his back.

Her protests echoed down the hallway. Only when it was silent did the guards release him.

The pavane ended. Behind him, the glass door opened, followed by the click of boot heels.

"My lord?" His valet's voice. "You are scheduled for the next dance. The lady awaits you."

He gritted his teeth. His mother meant well, but she had poor taste as a matchmaker. He summoned a smile and limped to the door.

The woman was dressed in white, of course, in a dress of startling simplicity, without the customary frippery. Then he saw her face, and he halted, stunned.

"Ella?"

She smiled, tentative, and curtseyed. "Hello, Your Highness."

"Saints above, Ella! What are you doing here?" He rushed inside to the heat and light. Courtiers mingled about in ivory and cream, but he saw only Ella. "And when did you stop calling me Roderick?"

Her mouth quirked up, and something in his chest unbunched. After all these years, her sense of humor remained. "I believe, Roderick, that I'm a surprise from your mother."

On the dais, his brother glared at them. His wife studied her lap, pretending as always not to exist. Another bruise the size of William's fist colored her cheek. But the queen mother watched the crowd expectantly--it was just like her to recall

Ella in case a local woman failed to catch his fancy. His mother had always been maddeningly thorough in her campaigns.

"She never said! And I've been petitioning William for months, ever since Father died. He said it would take time." A lie, he realized. William had never intended to bring Ella home. He felt William's glare, his inherited need to squash any happiness in another. He turned away, refusing to let his brother ruin this, too.

Ella shrugged. "Like I said, a surprise."

"A wondrous surprise."

That smile again, tentative, as if she couldn't believe his joy. Puzzling. Why would she think him anything less than delighted?

"Do you want to dance?" he asked. "Or sit and talk or...?" He wasn't sure what was the proper thing to do with a woman who had reappeared as if by a miracle.

"No sitting!" She held up her hands in mock horror. "I've spent two weeks stuck in a carriage and only arrived here an hour ago. Dancing sounds divine."

So he took her hand, pressed it to reinforce his delight, and led her to the dance floor. Around them, courtiers murmured, taking note of the new woman with the unfashionable gown.

He wanted to take her in his arms, to whisper in her ear all the things he'd kept in his heart these seven years. Instead he waited, chafing at the pause as the other dancers took their place. He saw now the lines on her face, the scar on her cheek, the tuft of gray at her temple.

"Was it terribly difficult," he asked, "these past few years?"

"Yes." She studied him, searching his face as if it was not quite what she expected. "I could tell you about it later, if you want, but not now."

He had caused these, the scar, the lines, the gray. He couldn't prevent his father slapping her, couldn't prevent her exile. No wonder she was cool towards him.

He wondered then if she had only come because his mother summoned her. He couldn't blame her if it was true. Like his father, he'd hurt her, and no doubt he was destined to hurt her again.

"Are you," he asked, grasping for happier topics, "still raising hounds?"

"No." She swallowed, and his heart sank. "The abbey only had mutts. They

107

were good dogs, but I didn't have time to train them."

"Abbey?"

"The Sisters of Good Hope took me in, let me stay as a lay member."

"What—" he started, horrified. Not that she'd been at an abbey, but because the Sisters of Good Hope worked in cities. How had Ella survived without meadows or forests to run in with her hounds? No wonder her hair had turned gray.

Before he could think of a response, the music started, a waltz. Automatically he took the first step and found she still fit in his arms. She still held her head high, still moved with the leggy grace of a creature born to run. This was the woman who'd trained her dogs to sniff out chestnuts for him, who'd climbed the tree outside his room to deliver books when his father denied him the library, who'd stroked his hair as he thought thoughts against the king he never dared put into words.

"I'm glad you came," he said because he must. "I've missed you. The missing was as deep as winter, as unfading as holly."

She slanted him a look, questioning, probing. "I wasn't allowed to send letters, but I collected bits of plant lore from pilgrims who passed through. Did Father Jacob forward them on?"

"That was you? He never said."

"He was nervous, worried he'd get in trouble if anyone found out."

"I wish he'd said. Your notes were incredible. I—"

His knee buckled. With a gasp, he slammed into the floor. His hands snagged fabric. Pain spiked through his knee and his palms, and the sound of tearing cloth sliced through the music.

He staggered up.

Ella stood gaping at her gown. Half the skirt had torn away, leaving her hoops and pantaloons exposed.

Around them, dancers skittered to a halt. Someone snickered, low and thick. At that, Ella pressed her hands to her reddening cheeks.

Horror welled in his chest. He had never, not once, tread on a lady's skirt. To do so now in such an egregious way, and to Ella—

"Ella," he whispered. He limped a painful step forward. "I'm so sorry."

But she was already turning away. Without a look back, without a word, she pushed through the crowd. How she must hate him.

On the dais, William smirked.

Roderick couldn't breathe. He clenched his fists.

A lady sidled up to him. "It's not your fault, Your Highness," she simpered. It was the one from earlier, the one with lashes like shadows. "She obviously tripped you. And no wonder, with how poorly she dances."

"Only a simpleton would blame you," another lady declared, stepping close. "Do you need a partner to finish the dance?"

"No!" He pushed his way through an encroaching swarm of white and ivory gowns. Was his mother already pushing court ladies on him again? "Let me through. Do not speak ill of her."

Ella was nowhere to be seen.

"Where did she go?" he demanded of his valet.

"I don't know, Your Highness. Should I have her found?"

He hesitated. William was gleeful on the dais, and having Ella returned would dampen that glee. But she was not Roderick's to drag back.

"No." A coldness hardened in his chest. "I have hurt her enough already."

The tapestry still hung in the library, but he was no longer a child who could hide behind it. He limped to the balcony, stood beside his bench. The evergreens fanned out below him: spruce, fir, juniper. How he envied them. They never hurt. They never hurt others. They stood still and quiet and cold.

But he no longer wanted that, he realized. Ella had been his once, and he had not fought for her. He would fight for her now, defy his brother, but would she accept him? Hadn't she just shown she wanted nothing to do with him?

He turned his back on his trees and strode past his valet, past the women in white who called to him.

Where would she go? Her guest room, most likely. But if his mother had craftily lodged her close to his suites, that room was halfway across the castle. Too far to go with torn skirts. The sitting rooms off the grand staircase then, the closest place that would give her privacy.

He limped down the grand staircase, its curling banister cold beneath his fingers. A shoe sat in the doorway of the first sitting room, wedged there to prop the door ajar. It was a white, flimsy thing, the fabric so sheer it might have been made of glass. He frowned at it. He'd never considered women's footwear before. If all lady's shoes were like this, no wonder Ella often preferred to go barefoot. Had she kicked this one off in disgust?

He knocked and recognized her voice.

A chill greeted him as he pushed the door open. The servants had neglected the fire, and Ella sat on a stool before the cold cinders, her torn skirts knotted in one fist.

"Oh, it's you." Her breath puffed while before her, and her surprise wounded him. Hadn't she thought he would come? "I thought—I was hoping a servant would come by with needle and thread."

"They're all busy upstairs. Shall I go find one?"

She nodded, and he turned to go, the shoe still in his hands. It shouldn't surprise him she thought him more useful when gone.

"Wait!"

Her cry stopped him. He looked back.

"Why didn't you come after me when your father exiled me?"

He sucked in his breath. The unrelenting winter of his longing surged hard in his chest. "You think I didn't want to? I didn't dream every day of riding to wherever you were, sweeping you off your feet?" The words, dammed for so long, poured out. "But my father said he would kill your papa and sisters if I did."

She covered her mouth with her free hand. "He said that?"

"He sent me an ear from one of the hounds you'd given him to reinforce the point. I couldn't do that to you."

She twisted her skirts in her hands. "Papa said not to contact you, but he never said why."

That sounded like her father, always trying to protect his children. Once again, Roderick wondered why *he* couldn't have been king.

"Still," she pressed, "you could have sent a letter or a message or something. I waited all those years."

"I sent word through the breeders network, but that didn't work." He hung his head. "I couldn't *find* you. No one who knew would tell me, and nothing I do is right—I couldn't even dance with you without tramping on your gown." His father's words echoed in his head: *Worthless boy! No one wants a weakling for a prince.*

Ella's mouth twisted. "Yes, it would have been better if you hadn't done that."

"And you're cold," he said, despairing. "Here I am talking, and you're cold." He held out the shoe to her.

She stuffed her hands under her arms. "Keep it. It's not comfortable, or warm. That's why I used it to prop the door."

"I'll find something." He looked around the room, but there was no blanket, not even a tapestry on the wall, and no tinderbox by the fire. Only a candle burned on a low table, and that would not help since they had no tinder. If he'd worn a cape he could have draped it over her shoulders, but he had only his tunic.

"It's all right—" she started.

"No," he said before she could tell him his failures were all right, she expected no more. "I'll find something. Wait here."

He set her shoe by her skirts and walked into the hallway. The corridors were deserted, filled only with the strains of harps and flutes from the ballroom. *Worthless, worthless,* his heart seemed to beat as he strode back up the stairs. He didn't want to go up to the ball and the simpering ladies in white, but this was for Ella, so he did.

At the top of the stairs he cornered a young page with an armload of candles. "Get a servant with needle and thread and a tinderbox to the sitting room off the staircase," he ordered. "Now."

The boy gawked at him. He'd probably never heard Roderick speak so forcefully. Then he bobbed his head and hurried off.

Roderick stole down a hallway, past courtiers who nodded to him, until he came to a guestroom, where he nicked a blanket off the bed and, just in case, stole the tinderbox from by the fireplace. He carried them down the staircase, wondering if he'd done enough. How could he prove his devotion to Ella? Could he ever do enough to make up for his past failings? And why should she accept him? He was destined to be as lonely and hurtful as William, wasn't he?

When he reached the bottom of the stairs, the sitting room door was ajar. He was sure he'd closed it, and he hurried forward, pleased that someone had attended to Ella so quickly.

He walked in on two guards in blue and silver.

"Come with us, miss," one said, taking Ella by the elbow. "His Majesty is worried about you having run off."

"I doubt he cares." Ella yanked her arm out of his grasp. "Can't I at least wait until my gown is properly patched?" She'd tied it closed as best she could with a ribbon from her hair, but there was no needle or thread yet.

"His Majesty—"

"Where are you taking her?" Roderick demanded.

The guards whirled about. Ella's eye lit up at the sound of his voice.

"Your Highness!" The other guard stepped towards him. "His Majesty asked us to find you, too. He's concerned—"

"It's been seven years!" Roderick bellowed. "My brother can't let us alone after seven years?"

The guards glanced at each other, eyes wide, but Roderick wasn't done.

"Did my brother specifically order you to bring us back? Did he command it as king?"

"Well, no." The second guard retreated a step. "He requested we find—"

"Then get out." Roderick hauled the guard's arm just as they'd tried to do to Ella. "We are not to be disturbed," he said as he steered the man into the hallway. "I command you to tell the king we'll return when we're ready, and he's not to disturb us before that. Understand?"

"Yes, my lord." The other guard scurried out before Roderick could grab him too. Roderick slammed the door.

He was breathing heavily. It was a night for firsts: stepping on a woman's gown, manhandling guards. He didn't like either, and the second had Ella staring at him as if she didn't recognize him.

"I'm sorry," he said, because it was what his father had taught him to say in any situation. He strode forward and draped the blanket around her shoulders.

"Don't be sorry. You were magnificent."

Roderick blinked. He could hardly believe what she had just said. But Ella never lied. She couldn't lie to his father, so she couldn't be lying now.

She scooted forward on her stool, drawing the blanket around her. "I needed to know you would come back for me, that you would fight for me."

"It was just some guards."

"Speaking in the king's name. You never would have defied that before."

"It's easier to be brave when you're with me," he said shyly.

"I know." She patted the stool beside her, but he held back.

He carried the tinderbox to the hearth, only there was already a little flame gaining strength there. It looked as if Ella had started the fire with a strip of cloth from her skirts and the candle. His shoulders slumped. She truly didn't need him.

"I've hurt you so many times," he said, laying the box on the mantle. "And I know I'll fail you again in the future. How can you want to be with me?"

"Your father hurt me," she said, emphasizing each word. "Just as he hurt you. But you never have, not intentionally, not maliciously, not like him."

"But—"

"No," she said. "I have always loved you because you were not like your father. You care for things, from saplings to dogs to barefoot girls from the north. Your father wouldn't care if I were cold, or if my skirts were torn, but you do. If you didn't, I'd have known you were no longer the man I loved. I would have marched from this palace and left you, guards and flimsy shoes be damned."

"That," he said softly, "I can believe."

"And now I know you're becoming the man you always wanted to be—a man who can stand up to guards, who can stake a claim against the king. We need that if we're to build a life together."

He nodded and found himself standing a bit taller.

"We shouldn't throw away our chance at happiness over a torn gown." She plucked at her skirts, tied closed with a bit of ribbon. "One thing I learned at the abbey was how to do for myself when needed. I know how to cobble things back together."

He smiled, small and sad. "I don't think I'm made for happiness."

She pressed her lips together. Sympathy lay there, and tenderness. If she could, he guessed, she would snip out the part of his life where his father had been and reassemble his life without the king. But that lay beyond the skills of even the most talented women.

"Do you think" she asked, "that you could aim for next to happy?"

He nudged the cast off shoe at her feet. How ridiculously flimsy it was. He would never think to dance in it, but someone had taken these airy bits and formed them into the semblance of a shoe. Maybe if tenuous bits of cloth could make the effort to be a shoe, he could make an effort at least to be content.

"Yes," he said. "I think I can try for that."

"Good." She cupped his cheek. "I can try for that, too."

He snagged her fingers. So warm. He bowed his head, rested his forehead against hers. She snuggled close until he held her in his arms. He wished he could remain there forever, just the two of them, a pocket of warmth in the world. "William won't be happy. He likes me unwed and childless."

"I know. But even he's not your father, and your mother is on our side. We'll find a way to manage him."

From upstairs, the music started again, a waltz. Upstairs, his valet would be waiting with another lady selected for this dance. Roderick had eyes only for the lady in front of him.

"Then, my dear," he said, "might we try another dance?" He held up her shoe.

"Maybe..." She raised the hem of her skirt. He slid the shoe into place. It fit perfectly. "If it involves waltzing outside to visit the kennels."

"But—don't you know? My father had them torn down. We board our hounds in town now."

"Oh." Her eyes went wide. Then she slanted him a smile. "Well, then, shall we look for a house in town near the kennels? Or pick a spot here to build new ones?"

"Now?"

"Why not? We'll never get back the years we lost. I don't intend to waste any that we have left."

"You'd be willing to live away from the palace?"

"Of course. Haven't you always wanted to?"

He glanced up at the ceiling, as if he could see where the king and the court were dancing. He could not escape all his responsibilities as prince, could never escape the memories that kept him up at night. But this evening, for once, he could do his best to forget. And in future, he could be the prince he needed to be at a distance.

He grinned. "Let's do both. There's some good land on the other side of town, beyond the pheasant fields. It'd be perfect for a house and new kennels. Want to see?"

"Lead the way."

He took her hand. "Let's find you good boots and a coat."

They went out together, the two of them, past the lonely evergreens, to see what life they could rebuild.

Kathryn Yelinek's story "Cinders and Snow" was published in Metaphorosis on Friday, 28 December 2018.

About the story

"Cinders and Snow" was inspired by events in the life of someone I know, but the details are not mine to share. Suffice it to say I've known several people who would never describe themselves as princes (of any gender), but who are the gentlest, most caring people I know—certainly princes (of any gender) in all the right ways. These people have overcome personal hardships that might have broken me, but they survived and thrived. I wanted to put a character like that into the traditional role of prince, but such a story didn't feel right with a traditional "the prince rescues the girl and they all live happily ever after" ending, because the effects of abuse can last a lifetime. Instead I went for a story where the two characters— prince and his lady love—rescue each other and live "next to happy" ever after.

A question for the author

Q: Do you write with a particular audience in mind?

A: Short answer: Yes, an audience of one—me.

Long answer: I don't start a story thinking, is this a story for young adults or adults? Or is this a story for people who like epic fantasy or urban fantasy or fairy tale retellings? My reading tastes encompass all of these subcategories, and I suspect the same is true of many readers. So I set out to write stories that I would want to read and that involve elements that are of interest to me. Of course this means I often write about similar concepts or themes. I'm a big bird-lover, so many of my stories involve birds to some degree. I once had a writer friend tell me that any story I write isn't one of mine unless it has a bird in it. I also tend to write about issues of loneliness, love, animal-human relations, and the environment. My stories often have at least a suggestion of happiness in the ending, if not a completely happy ending. I hope these elements appeal to a wide audience.

About the author

Kathryn Yelinek works as a librarian in Pennsylvania. In addition to the required hobbies of reading and writing, she enjoys bird watching, star-gazing, gardening, and going to see Broadway musicals. She and her husband share their home with one adorable parakeet, whom they are actively striving to make into the most spoiled bird in the Western Hemisphere. The bird doesn't seem to mind. Her works has appeared in

Daily Science Fiction, Deep Magic, Metaphorosis, Andromeda Spaceways Magazine, and *Beneath Ceaseless Skies.*

kathrynyelinek.com

Copyright

Metaphorosis Publishing

Metaphorosis offers beautifully written science fiction and fantasy. Our projects include:

Metaphorosis Magazine

Metaphorosis, a weekly magazine of SFF short stories, including stories from all the authors in this anthology. Find out more at magazine.metaphorosis.com, and sign up to be notified of new stories.

Metaphorosis Books

Recent books from Metaphorosis can be found at <u>books.metaphorosis.com</u>, and include:

Metaphorosis 2017   **Metaphorosis 2016**

All the stories from *Metaphorosis* magazine's second year.

Almost all the stories from *Metaphorosis* magazine's first year.

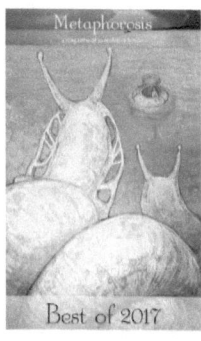

Metaphorosis:
Best of 2017

The best science
fiction and fantasy
stories from
Metaphorosis' 2nd
year.

Metaphorosis:
Best of 2016

The best science
fiction and fantasy
stories from
Metaphorosis' 1st
year.

Reading 5X5

Reading 5X5

Five stories, five times

Writers' Edition

Twenty-five SFF authors, five base stories, five versions of each – see how different writers take on the same material.

All the stories from the regular, readers' edition, plus two extra stories, the story seed, and authors' notes.

Best Vegan SFF of 2017

The best vegan science fiction and fantasy stories of 2017!

Best Vegan SFF of 2016

The best vegan science fiction and fantasy stories of 2016!

Susurrus

A darkly romantic story of magic, love, and suffering.

www.ingramcontent.com/pod-product-compliance
Lightning Source LLC
Chambersburg PA
CBHW020529120726
47904CB00003B/1014